MW01115281

CLEVER
Invites Someone New

Bob Hartman
Illustrated by Steve Brown

DAVID C COOK®

transforming lives together

CLEVER CUB INVITES SOMEONE NEW
Published by David C Cook
4050 Lee Vance Drive
Colorado Springs, CO 80918 U.S.A.

Integrity Music Limited, a Division of David C Cook
Brighton, East Sussex BN1 2RE, England

The graphic circle C logo is a registered trademark of David C Cook.

All Scripture paraphrases are based on the ESV® Bible (The Holy Bible, English
Standard Version®), copyright © 2001 by Crossway, a publishing ministry of
Good News Publishers. Used by permission. All rights reserved.

Library of Congress Control Number 2022946445
ISBN 978-0-8307-8471-4
eISBN 978-0-8307-8638-1

© 2023 Bob Hartman
Illustrations by Steve Brown. Copyright © 2023 David C Cook

The Team: Laura Derico, Stephanie Bennett, Judy Gillispie, James Hershberger, Susan Murdock

Cover Design: James Hershberger
Cover Art: Steve Brown

Printed in China
First Edition 2023

1 2 3 4 5 6 7 8 9 10

012723

"I cannot **WAIT** for my birthday party!" Clever Cub shouted. He was so excited, he threw his pinecones high!

"Who will you invite?" Mama Bear asked.

"Fred the bunny, of course!" Clever Cub said. "And Skippy Squirrel. And Dottie Deer. And …"

"What about someone from that **NEW** family in the forest?" Mama Bear suggested.

Clever Cub looked surpised and then wrinkled up his nose.
"The **STINKY** family? I don't think so!"

"That's not nice, Clever Cub." Mama Bear looked disappointed.

5

"No-o-o! That is their *real* name! Fred told me. Stinky Stinky is my age. His bigger brother is Quite Stinky. His next brother is called Very Stinky. And his biggest brother is called Super Stinky. Oh, and his little sister is called Rosey."

"Well, it would be nice to welcome Stinky and his family to the forest," Mama Bear said.

"But I do not KNOW him!" Clever Cub moaned. "What if he really is, you know, STINKY?"

6

"Hmm," Mama Bear said. "I know a Bible story you might need to hear." Clever Cub **LOVED** Bible stories. He sat down to listen.

"This story is about a man called Zacchaeus (zak-KEE-us)—a man **NOBODY** liked."

"Because he was stinky?" Clever Cub asked.

"No-o-o." Mama Bear shook her head. "Because he was a tax collector, and sometimes he took more money from people than he should have."

9

"He was a **ROBBER**?" Clever Cub's eyes got big.

"Sort of," Mama Bear said. "He was a cheater. But one day he heard that Jesus was coming to visit Jericho, the town where Zacchaeus lived. Everyone wanted to see Jesus, so they went out to wait for Him along the road."

"Even Zacchaeus?" Clever Cub asked.

"Even Zacchaeus," Mama Bear said. "But because he was short, he could not see over the crowd. And because no one liked him, they wouldn't let him stand in the front."

Clever Cub scratched his nose. He always did that when he was thinking. "What did he do?"

"He was very **CLEVER**—a bit like a little bear I know." Mama Bear smiled at her cub. "And he was good at climbing trees."

"Also like a little bear you know!" Clever Cub added.

"Indeed!" Mama Bear laughed. "Zacchaeus climbed up a sycamore-fig tree. From there, he could see the road, but the people couldn't see *him*."

13

"When Jesus came into town, *everyone* wanted to talk to Him. But Jesus kept walking. He knew there was one person in that crowd who needed a **FRIEND** very much that day.

"Then Jesus came to the sycamore-fig tree. He looked up, up, **UP** and said, 'Zacchaeus! Come down! I want to stay at your house today.'"

"Wow! Was Zacchaeus surprised?" Clever Cub asked.

"He was," Mama Bear said. "And the crowd was surprised too. 'Zacchaeus is a bad man. He's a cheater,' they muttered. 'Why is Jesus going to *his* house?'"

"I know why!" Clever Cub shouted.
"Because Jesus is a friend to everyone!"

"Yes, He is." Mama Bear continued the story. "Zacchaeus came down, down, **DOWN** out of that tree. He welcomed Jesus to his house. Then something else happened ..."

"Zacchaeus felt sorry for all the bad things he had done. He called out so **EVERYONE** could hear. 'Look! I will give half my money to the poor. And I will pay back anyone I have cheated—even four times the amount!'"

"**WOW**! Another surprise!" Clever Cub shouted.

"Indeed." Mama Bear nodded. "Then Jesus said to the crowd, 'Today, this man has been saved from the bad things he has done. Welcome him, for he is a part of your community! I have come to invite everyone to be a part of God's family.'"

"Hmm." Clever Cub was thinking. He scratched his nose. "So, no one liked Zacchaeus. But Jesus looked for him and welcomed him. And then *everyone* welcomed him?"

"That's right, Clever Cub!" Mama Bear smiled. "When people feel loved by Jesus, it changes **EVERYTHING**. And *we* can show Jesus' love to others too."

"Like to Stinky?" Clever Cub asked.

21

"Yes, exactly!" Mama Bear said.

22

"All right! I'll go look for him now. Maybe I'll find him in a **TREE!**"
And Clever Cub took Fred with him to go find the whole Stinky
family and invite them to his party.

For Clever Readers

Clever Cub is a curious little bear who **LOVES** to cuddle up with the Bible and learn about God! Clever Cub didn't want to invite Stinky the skunk to his birthday party. But Mama Bear told him what happened when Jesus invited Zacchaeus (from Luke 19:1–10)— everything changed for good! And Clever Cub decided that inviting Stinky might be good too.

If you had a party, who would you want to come? Jesus invites everyone to live in God's kingdom. He wants to be a friend to everyone. Maybe someone you know needs a friend too. Who could you invite to be your friend today?